S.S. SAN PEDRO

Books by James Gould Cozzens

S.S. SAN PEDRO
1931

THE LAST ADAM
1933

CASTAWAY
1934

MEN AND BRETHREN
1936

ASK ME TOMORROW; OR YOUNG FORTUNATUS
1940

THE JUST AND THE UNJUST
1942

GUARD OF HONOR
1948

BY LOVE POSSESSED
1957

CHILDREN AND OTHERS
1964

JAMES GOULD COZZENS

S.S. San Pedro

HARCOURT, BRACE & WORLD, INC., NEW YORK

C 882 ω2

R 4 Aω

LIBRARY OF CONGRESS CATALOG CARD NUMBER: 67-19206

PRINTED IN THE UNITED STATES OF AMERICA

S.S. SAN PEDRO

ONE

June 7, Friday, in the morning, the twin-screw turbine liner *San Pedro,* seventeen thousand tons, lay at her Hoboken pier. To sail at noon on Brixton & Heath's Brazil–River Plate express service, she bore a million dollars in gold for the banking houses of the Argentine. Lashed on her forward well-deck, wedged in number one and number two upper holds, were automobiles, crated, for Montevideo. She carried two thousand tons of cash registers and baking-powder in tins, of cotton shirts and bathtubs, of children's toys, agricultural implements, and a sealed consignment of machine-guns for the government of Paraguay. Coal to bring her out and back loaded her down, overflowing into shelter-deck bunkers forward. Between ten o'clock and half past eleven she took on board one hundred and seventy-two passengers.

*

Aft, they had a boom out. Trunks were assembled by the half-ton in a corded net on the wharf floor. The boom picked them up easily, swung them into the blaze of the sun. They dropped down number six hatch to the baggage-rooms. Leaning on the rail of the light after-bridge, where he could watch from on high, waited Mr. Bradell, the senior second officer. Mr. Bradell's white-and-gold stood out clean on the heat-dulled blue. A seaman, also white-clad, scarlet semaphore flags thrust under his arm, waited with him, though they would not cast off, Miro knew, for almost an hour.

Miro, first quartermaster, was in direct charge on deck. Miro was Brazilian, coffee-colored from the intense sun and his mixture of bloods, Indian and Negro. Clear and cheerful-eyed, his sound white teeth flashing, his head, erect, covered by a mat of strong black curls which sweat had dampened, he was watching paternally over Packy, the big Jamaican Negro at the winch. Packy was dead drunk, unable to speak, but he remained mechanically precise. He and the winch met at an abysmal level of brainless strength. Like the boom on its gooseneck, Packy pivoted blindly on the small hard point of habit. Like the boom, he described invariably the same controlled semicircles.

Miro stayed behind him in case he should fall unconscious. He was the only person who could manage Packy, and managed by Miro, Packy was perfection. The quartermaster told him so from time to time, in the rich chant of the black lingua franca of the islands. It was equivalent to oil in Packy's bearings and Packy was all right.

4

Confirming this, Miro shot his eyes up to the white skeleton of the after-bridge, thin on the blue; an eloquent glance to Mr. Bradell, who answered it with a slight mute nod. Miro's whistle shrilled out then, the winch gasped and clanked, the shadow of the boom went swiftly over, the empty net collapsed on the wharf floor. Things were tight, smart, going as they should go.

It was, in Miro's idiom, a matter of *tela*. Integrate with the Spanish sense of tone, texture, woven firmness was the untranslatable value of a plan, a sustained argument underlying a mode of behavior. It was wide enough to include that beautiful gift of the white man, the disciplined coöperation, speed, and precision of people quick and certain about their duties. This abstraction was the last, perfect pleasure, epitomized by Mr. Bradell in attention alert and quiet above, but, in addition, that a man might know he was good flesh as well as blessed spirit, there were the white uniforms against the sky, the sharp stripe of color in the rolled signal-flags, the smell of hot tar, hot metal, hot salt, of steam and oil and warm wet hemp.

Miro blew on his whistle, jubilant. From his pocket he took out a big gold watch covered with engraved scrolls, a piece of a ruby set on top the stem, fastened to a gold fob, and its magnificence testified to him again the rightness of the world. He worked long and saved, he was quick and quiet, he did not do every foolish thing he thought of, and in the end, with his own money, he could buy such a watch. He looked at it now and noted that it was exactly eleven o'clock. The tugs, he

5

saw, were already off the end of the pier, and with the pleasure of going so soon seaward, he put the watch carefully away, happier if possible than he had been. To Packy he began to sing, throaty and soft, "Hail, Mary, full of grace . . ."

At five minutes past eleven Miro's intelligent eye caught the flicker of the signalman's flags, gay against the serene heavens, answering the navigating bridge. Mr. Bradell turned. He came handily down the ladder, crossing over into the shadows. To Miro he said: "Mr. Fenton will stand by here."

The fourth officer was even then descending from the promenade-deck. Mr. Bradell spoke to him a moment before he mounted quickly out of Miro's sight.

Anthony Bradell, passing the smoking-room doors, avoided the approving glances of two girls. His brown face, at once too thin, too bluntly shaped for any handsomeness, looked none the less like the passenger's idea of a navigating officer. He knew the girls were still watching him as he climbed again to the boat-deck. From the bridge end the quartermaster on duty there hailed him as he came closer. "Captain Clendening in his cabin, Mr. Bradell."

Anthony passed the windows of the wireless-room, saw the first and second operators playing checkers, and raised his hand to the red-headed one. At the passage-door forward he reached in and knocked up the hook which held it ajar. On the captain's door he rapped sharply.

In Captain Clendening's cabin an electric fan vibrated. A tepid shaft of air twitched left to right in a slow arc from the high corner. The captain's radio, muted down, recited intricate directions for some sort of cooking. He must have forgotten to turn it off, not noticing.

Heavy in his white-and-gold, Captain Clendening sat in the swivel chair, back to his desk. He was feeling the terrible waterside heat, Anthony decided, for the captain looked obscurely pale. Wind, tan, years of exposure had given his face a permanent rich color, but this lay now over his cheeks like a surface veneer. Clinging to the sides of his head, his hair, usually a harsh white fur, looked weak and damp. His old blue eyes, always marred by a droop on the left, were unnaturally listless. An early injury to his jaw—Anthony had heard that it was from a thrown marline-spike—made itself felt more and more as the captain grew older, and most today. His right brow arched up round and steep; the left lay flat. The left corner of the mouth sank in a lump outstanding toward the stubborn chin. Over his mouth, strongly set even in this sag, he grew a short mustache, white, like the fur along his head. He looked at Anthony with an obvious sharp approval.

"Mr. Bradell, our senior second officer," he said, addressing the man on the settee along the wall. "Only sailor on board, God help him. Had his master's papers five years. Just waiting for me to die so the company will have a ship for him." His voice rumbled authentically, but the unwieldy humor was flattened, almost exhausted. It would be impudent, as well as unthinkable, Anthony admitted, to suggest that Mr. Driscoll, the chief officer,

7

be allowed to take the *San Pedro* out. Fortunately ignorant of his thought, Captain Clendening continued: "Bradell, my friend Doctor Percival wants to look the ship over. You can show him about, I guess. Fenton get aft all right?"

"Yes, sir," said Anthony at once. He was blank with astonishment at the inopportunity of the request and he turned sharply toward this man for whom the captain was willing to upset all reasonable routine.

Doctor Percival sat quiet, looking back at Anthony with an accurate, absorbed attention. Doctor Percival's tight face was fleshless and almost gray. His lips sank in, rounded over his teeth. They were lips so scanty that you could see the line of the teeth meeting. His eyes, red-rimmed, lay limp in their sockets, appearing to have no color at all. Doctor Percival's intense pale gaze came out of holes covered with soft, semitransparent lenses. His head, one observed, jolted, was utterly hairless, and a pale-reddish star, a mark like a healed wound, lay across the crown. Every modulation of bone showed through a sere leaf of old skin.

Doctor Percival recognized Anthony's instinctive recoil from this fearful face, and just as obviously prepared to overlook it, indifferent, but he was betrayed by a sudden muscular movement. The whole hollow countenance winced a little; the lips twitched wide in a grimace most like a broken and derisive smile. Anthony stood frozen, for Doctor Percival's eyes denied the expression any significance. It was involuntary; it might, Anthony saw, happen again at any moment. Doctor Percival, with a dignity terrible and silent, held out a gray

8

glove whose palm was dark with moisture. Anthony took it in his own bare brown hand, which he closed hard on the slight, cloth-covered fingers. It was a grip half iron and bone-breaking, but Doctor Percival did not appear to notice. Anthony leveled his gaze out, made his brown eyes look straight into Doctor Percival's colorless ones, and said: "Glad to show you around, Doctor Percival."

He turned at once and opened the door. If he did not feel well, the captain had seen more than enough of that face. Thinking so, Anthony was embarrassed to realize that Doctor Percival somehow understood him, as though he had spoken every word aloud. Doctor Percival was shaking hands with the captain. He said in an exact, highly educated voice: "Take care of yourself until I see you again, John. There is nothing you need to do now." He put his shabby black hat on, stepping out into the passage. Captain Clendening merely nodded. "Good of you to come down, doctor," he said. "Go aft when you finish, Bradell," he added. "Don't like to leave that boy there alone."

Doctor Percival had turned, defeating absolutely Anthony's desire to bring him out on the sunny deck. They went together down the inside stairs at the end. Anthony asked carefully: "What would you like to see, sir?"

He attracted to himself that acute gaze. "I really do not know," Doctor Percival said. "It is some time since I have been on a ship—" It was coming, Anthony saw. The broken smile made a kind of irrelevant joke of his

9

last words. Anthony tightened his lips, expressionless.

In the silence ensuing, Doctor Percival, his voice low, said: "But you do not float quite level, do you?"

Astonished, Anthony noticed for the first time that they had, in fact, a slight port list. "We straighten up when we get under way," he said. "We can correct it with the ballast-tanks."

"No danger of tipping over?" asked Doctor Percival.

"Oh, no," said Anthony. "When we're heavily loaded it takes a little adjustment."

"Many passengers?" asked his companion. His voice faded to a husky whisper.

"I don't know exactly," Anthony said, resisting the natural temptation to speak low in return. "I should say a hundred and fifty or more."

"And how many men to run the boat?"

"You mean officers?"

"Altogether."

"Oh, we have a crew of two hundred odd."

"Then you carry perhaps four hundred people? It must be a great responsibility?"

Anthony said: "We try to take care of them."

They had been advancing through an alleyway, going aft, which led them out by the purser's office in the main entry. Here it was crowded, confused and noisy.

"The purser's office," Anthony explained needlessly. "The lounge, the public rooms, and so on are above. The dining-room is below there."

Doctor Percival nodded slowly. He looked about him with meticulous attention. He might have been afraid that he was going to overlook something of real importance. "These are passengers, I suppose?" he said.

"Mostly," said Anthony.

"Ah," said Doctor Percival. Anthony snapped his eyes away, detecting the start of that horrid trembling about the mouth. Doctor Percival, he knew now, could not continue speaking until it was past. Anthony had time to notice again the two girls who had admired him aft. One of them was going to smile this time, so he looked back to Doctor Percival. Other people had begun to observe them, considering Doctor Percival's fleshless face and shabby clothes with a sort of electric consternation. Anthony exerted a slight pressure on his companion's arm. "We can go down to the dining-room," he said.

Doctor Percival said: "It would be interesting to see them all eating."

"Oh, they're not eating now," Anthony said. "They don't serve luncheon until after we sail." Anxious to get Doctor Percival out of the lobby, he had been prepared to assist him downstairs. The firmness of the man's step abashed him. Doctor Percival, Anthony realized, was not exactly old. He was simply not young. And far from being weak, he had an unexpected inert strength. His steps fell heavy as stones, despite his slight appearance.

"This is the dining-room," said Anthony.

"Ah," said Doctor Percival, "that is interesting. Would it be possible to see the machinery?"

Anthony hesitated at the dining-room doors. Here the

chief steward was assigning tables to a line of people waiting, and all these seemed to turn at once, attracted by those steps on the stairs. They gaped at Doctor Percival. "Yes," said Anthony, deciding to risk Mr. MacGillivray's annoyance, if only he could get his companion out of the way somewhere. "We could stop in a moment. We could look at the engines from above. They're pretty busy now, of course."

They went down the alleyway. "We just step in here," Anthony said. "I'm afraid you'll be pretty warm, sir. Would you like to take your overcoat off?"

"No, no," said Doctor Percival. "I don't feel heat."

Anthony twisted the iron handle. Up to them almost overwhelming came the hot oily breath, the surge of sound in the engine-room shaft. Anthony closed the door and they stood together on the landing outside the chief engineer's office. Anthony glanced in fleetingly, saw Mr. MacGillivray sitting at his desk, the shirt on his back soaked with patches of sweat, his sleeves rolled up on his big freckled arms. He was busy with papers.

Doctor Percival put his gloved hands on the rail.

"That's dirty, I'm afraid, sir," said Anthony, raising his voice. "There really isn't much to see. They're warming up the turbines now. Those are the turbines there, those big green things."

"Ah," nodded Doctor Percival. Anthony's face hardened, but he held his eyes unwavering. "They supply the power, I presume," Doctor Percival said when it was over. His harsh whisper was entirely clear, neither lower nor louder than it had seemed outside.

"Of course, there's an astern turbine, too," Anthony shouted. "Not much to see—"

The chief was coming out of his office. He paused, surprised, and stared at Anthony coldly. "Just showing a friend of the captain's what we've got," Anthony said. "Doctor Percival, this is Mr. MacGillivray, the chief engineer."

Mr. MacGillivray gave him one steady look. He put out a hand with enlarged knuckles covered by loose freckled skin and hosts of pale hairs. He closed it like a trap on Doctor Percival's glove. "Sorry I haven't more time," he said briefly. Disturbing his resemblance to a mild and friendly bloodhound, his face began to harden. It hung free from the cheek-bones, but stiffly now. In the folds, stubbled with two days' blond beard, his mouth was usually lost. Now his lips pouted out solidly. Pale china blue, his eyes peered with a candid dislike beneath his big brows. Even the skin of his forehead, white from three decades under electric lights, colored a little in gathering irritation.

Doctor Percival ignored this change. "Are they very powerful?" He made a fragmentary gesture toward the turbine cases.

After a while Mr. MacGillivray roared: "Oh, we get twelve thousand shaft horse-power." He started brusquely to go down the steps. Then he halted. He made it plain that he considered this visitor an emergency requiring his presence. He waited while Doctor Percival neither said anything nor moved. Finally Mr. MacGillivray raised a hand and shouted: "Mr. Forsay! Ask can we try!"

Below, a head in a dirty white cap which had been studying the micrometers tilted up a face and yelled back: "Ask to try, sir." It turned then and bent over the desk toward the bridge telephone.

"What is it you are going to do now?" Doctor Percival asked.

"See if we work," said the chief bluntly.

"Try away, sir!" sang up the voice.

"Port engine, Mr. Forsay!"

"Port engine, sir."

"They always do work, I suppose," said Doctor Percival. He removed his hat and Mr. MacGillivray almost stepped back, seeing the hairless skull and the jagged reddish star. "Never know till they do," he said, swallowing.

The three of them stood there, staring down in silence, as though they awaited a sign or a miracle. A bell clashed out; simultaneously signal-lights winked red. At once, like the first man breathed on by God, the *San Pedro* was coming alive. From her own boilers the unspeakable breath of superheated steam inspired her. Strong as ten thousand horses it broke out in the steel vitals of the port turbine. With stunning impact, it ricocheted, smashing off the stationary vanes. It impinged like a hundred sledge-hammers on the converse rotor blades. Now, you might think, the *San Pedro* contracted its mighty muscles and girded its loins. The shaft-barrel, locked in the ponderous triple grip of the balancing pistons, steadied to a frustrated quiver. It strained titanically. It yielded. Twisting their film of oil to a lather, the journal-bearings revolved. The great thrust-

14

bearing braced in obdurate mastery. Far astern, dim in the water beyond the hull, over went the big blades of the port-propeller. The *San Pedro* winced ahead in her moorings.

Mr. MacGillivray turned his eyes coldly on Doctor Percival. "They work," he said, and while he spoke Doctor Percival's face twitched, the mouth broke to pieces. Mr. MacGillivray stared at him.

"Port engine okay, sir," shouted up Mr. Forsay.

"You a passenger?" asked Mr. MacGillivray, paying no attention.

"No," said Doctor Percival. He opened the door himself and stepped into the alleyway.

"Listen!" Mr. MacGillivray roared to Anthony. "Don't you know any better than to bring these dumbbells in when we're warming up, son? Down here, we work. And furthermore, I don't like your friend. Now, get out!"

Anthony stepped, flushed and warm, into the alleyway, too. He closed the door. Doctor Percival was looking at him with absorbed colorless attention, and Anthony said, flustered: "The chief's pretty sharp-tongued. He doesn't mean anything, though."

Doctor Percival whispered: "I do not blame him. He has a great responsibility, after all, keeping those engines. You would be entirely helpless without them, wouldn't you?"

"We'd be in a bad way," Anthony said. "Did you say you wanted to go ashore, sir?"

They came up the stairs by the dining-room and

through the press of the main entry. The third officer was at the head of the gangway. He looked at Anthony and then at his companion and whistled soundlessly. "Ready to put off, Mr. Bradell," he said.

"Yes, I must go," said Doctor Percival. A light somewhat more distinct came into the pale holes of his lensed eyes. "The captain," he said very low to Anthony, "is an old man, Mr. Bradell."

"What did you say, sir?" asked Anthony, taken aback.

"People grow old, Mr. Bradell. They break down, they wear out."

"If you consider him worn out, sir," said Anthony sharply, "you're wrong. You can ask the ship's doctor about that."

"I have no interest in the opinion of ships' doctors," whispered Doctor Percival. He closed his eyes a moment. "I am merely mentioning a fact."

"It isn't my place to discuss anything like that with you, sir," said Anthony.

"This is not a discussion, Mr. Bradell," said Doctor Percival.

"I am afraid I must go," said Anthony.

"Yes," said Doctor Percival, unannoyed, "you must. So must I."

"Second gong's gone, Mr. Bradell," called the third officer, impatient.

Doctor Percival made no effort either to thank him or to shake hands. He had not halted a moment while he was speaking. Now his unhurried progress simply bore him on, leaving Anthony behind. The sun, slanting almost perpendicular between the edge of the wharf roof and the *San Pedro*'s side, lay hot on the slope of the gangplank. Doctor Percival's black figure moved there, passed on; was lost in deep shadows ashore.

The third officer whistled again, audibly this time. Anthony turned aft to take over Mr. Fenton's charge.

In the sun of the deck below he passed Miro and the carpenter's mate busy with the hatch covers. At the top of the ladder Mr. Fenton touched his cap smartly. The semaphore flags awoke on the navigating bridge. "We'll cast off," nodded Anthony. Mr. Fenton said: "We've got quite a list, haven't we?"

"Straighten it up under way—" Anthony started to say, but the great rising roar of the *San Pedro*'s whistle drowned him out.

TWO

STEADY AND STRONG through the infinite ocean twilight the *San Pedro* maintained her seventeen knots. The vital quiver of her engines gave her a mounting wave of vibration, like a piano feeling the pedal. Her warm untroubled breath trembled up her shafts and ventilators. She was calm in the lucid radiance of her early lights. Around the dining-room a whole half-deck of her stirred with more intense activity. In the balcony the orchestra was gathering; by the buffet the chief steward was checking the flowers on the many tables. He made a sign to his assistant that the doors might be opened when he heard the gong. Aft, the smoking-room was murmuring, expansive in crowded comfort; ice rattled in the bright bar; mild air moved in the doors open on the deck behind. Seen from here, the smoke-soiled mast with the hidden glow of the running light, the booms laid down, the dim sunset radiance remaining on the steerage superstructure, all rose and fell together gently. Astern, the quiet ocean, neither blue nor black, extended in limitless ease to the faintly colored horizon, darkening now to evening at the end of the *San Pedro*'s steady white wake.

On the navigating bridge, Mr. Eberly, the junior second officer, had the watch. A helmsman was planted at the wheel. A quartermaster with folded arms stared away into the dusk beside him. In the chart-room behind, Captain Clendening wrote the night orders under the glow of a green-shaded lamp. Calculations from the wireless-room informed him of the vessels to be met or overtaken before morning, and the approximate times they would come abreast. He noted them down one after another as a caution to the watch-officer. Many of these ships he knew; on two of them the masters were old acquaintances.

Thinking about these friends, he wrote more slowly. The overwhelming monotony and weariness of the sea weighed him down. Bound north, bound south, the same ships, the same men were always passing. On his own ship, when he went to dinner, passengers impossible to distinguish from a thousand others, doubly regimented by what the company considered importance, would be at his table—all the same; only their names were different. In many cases even the names might be the same and he must recall previous voyages, details of personality and business. He pressed the buzzer. The quartermaster came, took the sheet and posted it on the bridge board. Muffled, the metallic throb of the hammered dinner-gong rose, but Captain Clendening remained motionless, wondering how many more voyages he would be good for, and what would be left then but death, so slow, so horribly swift.

Below, on the engine-room shaft, Mr. MacGillivray sat in his office. He was vigorously scrubbed and shaved. His uniform coat was buttoned neatly over his round belly. He wore a low stiff collar and a black silk tie. While he glanced at the afternoon reports he cleaned his fingernails, digging slowly and methodically with a pocket-file. Placid, clean, and comfortable, he was pleased at the thought of a tableful of new people who would presently await him in the dining-room. He took time to rehearse one or two of the suitable anecdotes which had served him well on twenty trips. All the while up to him poured the fine steam and steel symphony of full-ahead. His big ears, with the pale blond hairs growing out of them, cocked to it invisibly, he was exhilarated by the perfect correctness of its blended noises. In his mind's eye this peace of good performance took the envisioned shape of the long submarine shaft alleys, their spaced electric lights winking on the great shafts revolving. Liquid with oil, brighter than silver, they spun serenely on their bearings, ninety times a minute.

The dinner-gong aroused him and he arose contentedly, giving his nails one last critical inspection. He stopped and waved his hand to the watch-officer below to show that he was leaving. Then he pulled in his stomach as far as it would go, straightened his shoulders. His face began to beam with urbane anticipation: and out he went, sedately.

In the fire-room, like almost heroic figures against the hell of the swung-open doors, the black gang stood to its furnaces. Wheelbarrows from the bunker chutes rattled on the steel flooring. Covers rang successively shut. The chief fireman swigged down a half-pint of tepid tea, retaining some of it to spit sizzling on the hot iron. Swinging his gorilla arms, rolling up his eyes, the crazy man called Quail balanced on his shovel handle and began to intone hoarse organ notes which suddenly merged into the "St. Louis Blues." The Haitian Negroes simply stared at him, but those from the Barbados and Jamaica had picked up the words and felt the long sad pull of the music. They wiped their foreheads and raised their voices. The chief fireman said: "Never mind that, Bo! All you got to do is work." But there was no sense in trying to tell Quail anything. The only things he could understand, he knew already—food, liquor, and shoveling. Just under the roar of the fans, the forced drafts, and the clamor of the moving machinery their chant rose in a musical thick moan, a muffled lament fading between the great overjutting boilers. The chief fireman, his eyes sternly on the dials, gave way after a moment and moaned with them.

In his cabin Anthony Bradell was shaving. His face was half covered with lather and he held his razor motionless from time to time, listening to Miro, who stood stiffly in the corner at a sort of attention. Miro continued: "Six four are twenty-four; six five are thirty; six six are forty-two—"

"Try again," said Anthony.

"Thirty-six, sir," responded Miro, inspired. He had been many months on the multiplication tables, for he could see no reason to hurry. Mr. Bradell thought a quartermaster ought to be working for a third mate's license, but Miro knew it would be useless to him, since he meant to remain in Brixton & Heath's employ as long as Mr. Bradell was on a Brixton & Heath ship. The company could never advance anyone with Negro blood. Miro understood this perfectly and it did not trouble him, for he had no desire to be advanced. Life gave him now everything he wanted and penalized him not at all. He even enjoyed trying to learn mathematics, not through any desire to determine latitude by meridian altitude, but because such activity was *tela;* something stern and difficult to be done, unspoiled by any completion or end in view. In time, if Mr. Bradell's patience should seem to wear thin, he would make an effort for Mr. Bradell's sake and submit to examinations. He was not alarmed at the possibility of passing. Mr. Bradell would not want him to stop there. The requirements for a second mate's papers might legitimately be made into the work of centuries. Miro could, he was calmly sure, never learn anything about longitude by chronometer. Deviation of the compass by an amplitude or an azimuth would be certainly impossible. He must be old, probably dead, before he satisfied Mr. Bradell about them. Concluding his recitation he smiled eloquently and said: "I will study them again, sir."

"It will come easier," said Anthony, who thought he might be discouraged. "Better turn in now. You've had a hard day."

"Good night, sir," said Miro. He was happy to have made so little progress. "Thank you very much, sir."

There was starlight on the forward deck. Here Miro leaned a moment on the rail, feeling the moist wind in his face, watching the soft sea break open about the *San Pedro*'s advancing stem, filming up her prow and falling off. She was constructed with very little freeboard, so the water was close and fast. He noticed that she still listed slightly. This displeased him. As they said in the islands, where they had picked it up from the Royal Navy, it was not "tiddly."

He entered the door at last and went to find Packy. As he expected, Packy was half off his bunk. With a tolerant shove of his foot he pushed Packy securely against the wall, for he expected it to blow up before morning. Then he bent down and searched underneath until he found the corked gin bottle. This he took, to lock in his own box, so the boatswain would not find it and throw it overboard. Packy would need miserably one stiff drink some time during the forenoon. In a position to bargain with him, Miro could force Packy to assign him all his money. Then Packy, ashore in the South, could not get mixed up with some woman who might make him miss the boat.

In the quartermasters' bunk-room Miro stripped to his underwear, wrapped himself in a blanket, and lay staring up in the dim light. Contented, he recommended himself to the Cuban Virgin of Cobre, to San Juan de

Matha, and to San Pedro Tomás, all of whom had kindly superintended men at sea.

Left alone, Anthony Bradell finished his shaving. A fresh uniform lay on his bunk and he considered it without pleasure while he put away his shaving things, restoring his cabin to its brutally bare and immaculate good order. It was an idea of the company that some officers not on duty should go down after dinner when the passengers were dancing in the widened waist of the promenade-deck and make themselves agreeable. On most of the company's vessels leadership in this fell conveniently to the chief officer, who stood no watch. Mr. Driscoll of the *San Pedro* was not a success socially. Captain Clendening had selected Anthony instead. He did not, he told his senior second officer when he gave the order, know what the hell the sea had come to, but the *San Pedro* might as well make as good a showing as possible. Anthony could leave at ten o'clock, and he needn't come onto the morning watch until four bells on such nights. Mr. Fenton, who acted as his junior watch-officer, was perfectly competent. Anthony agreed about the fourth officer's competence. He did not consider sleep precisely a vice, but any concern about it failed to fit in with the efficient asceticism he had brought himself to practice. He would continue to be called as usual.

The captain, perfectly aware of this, added in a better temper that Anthony would report to the captain's cabin at ten. "First thing you know," he said with a grimly bawdy sardonicism, "you'll be up on the boat-deck with some little piece in skirts."

It was his method of chiding an exaggerated stiffness in Anthony's attitude. He drove the point home by pulling down from the small row of books the Revised Statutes. He bent the volume open to Section 280 and asked him ironically to consider the fate of the erring officer ". . . who 'during the voyage under promise of marriage, or by threats, or the exercise of authority, or solicitation—' that includes standing around in uniform, boy," he interpolated, "—'or the making of gifts or presents, seduces and has illicit connection with any female passenger, shall be fined not more than one thousand dollars or imprisoned for not more than one year. . . .' Or both," he added. "Hardly ever worth it."

Anthony agreed, with composure. Like himself, the captain was an inarticulate man. On the rare occasions when he chose to soften his formal attitude he could resort only to this gruff and tortuous humor. It expressed for him a paternal affection, of which his long training at sea made him instinctively avoid any show. Anthony, who was more attached to him and respected him more than any other human being, understood. Captain Clendening, knowing he did, put the relationship away with the book, snapped closed and returned to the shelf. "That's all, Mr. Bradell," he said. "I'll expect you to stand by below on quiet evenings."

Anthony said: "Yes, sir."

He had been doing it for over a year now. By degrees

his customary thoroughness made him an adequate dancer, but it was purely a matter of discipline. The fact remained that it was a silly thing for a seaman to be doing.

Tonight he considered with positive apprehension those two girls who had first seen him aft and then again with Doctor Percival in the entry. They would be enthusiastic dancers. He could only hope that during the afternoon they might have attached some desirable males who would monopolize them.

The watch had changed and Mr. Eberly, coming belatedly to his quarters, stuck in his round face and said: "Going to knock them dead, Bradell?"

This was perhaps the two hundred and fiftieth repetition of that question, so Anthony didn't think it needed an answer. Mr. Eberly usually came down himself and liked it, so Anthony said: "You'd better get going. You might miss some of it. Couple of kids I'm going to see you meet."

"Thanks," said Mr. Eberly. "Dumb-looking lot of women on this trip."

Dimly from the lower deck dance-music beat up now and Mr. Eberly withdrew. Anthony, severe and noncommittal, went out. At the wireless-room he paused. "What do you get?" he asked, standing into the light of the door.

Morris, the second operator, was on duty. A cigarette sagged out of the corner of his mouth. One of his headphones was pushed up, resting against his reddish hair. The other dug tight into his left ear. His pointed young face turned, flippant in profile, suiting itself to the unoriginal jargon of his ready mockery. He spoke at once, with the accent, jeering, tight-voweled, of poor Boston streets. "Plenty," he said. "Bad weather south. Force seven and getting worse. We'll catch it, I guess. Had the *San Pablo* for a few minutes. The old man wanted to know where they were. Finally got a QRN off them. You'd think they were in China. Tell your girl friends they'll all be sick tomorrow."

"Right with me," said Anthony. "Hurry it up if you can."

"You're just a minor error," said Morris. "I wish I could see some women without a grill to protect them."

Anthony moved down the deck. The *San Pedro's* funnel was steaming against the stars. He felt the warm blast of the engine-room shaft, and then the mild ocean air, as he turned in the stairs. Japanese lanterns had been strung along the deck. He advanced into this dusk, standing near the orchestra in the corner. The two girls, who had gotten into elaborate dinner-dresses, noticed him at once, but the press of people dancing interfered with their advance. They managed it gradually, around the edges, arm in arm, until they stood beside him with an appearance of accident so preposterous that Anthony groaned inwardly and gave way. "Nice evening, isn't it?" he said.

"Do you run this ship?" said the blond one engagingly. "Because, if you do, I wish you'd fix it."

"It's completely cock-eyed," her companion informed him, more calmly. "It doesn't sit straight. You don't notice it much until you try to dance. Then you just slide over to the rail."

Her eyebrows rose, miraculously slim and black. She used a heavy warm scent, some modification of the patchouli Anthony associated with the segregated districts of the Southern ports. She ought to be spanked, he decided, but he said in the manner he had developed for passengers: "I'll speak to the captain about it. I wouldn't be surprised if he had it fixed by morning."

He could dance with her, if he liked, she announced negligently. "Clara won't mind. There comes her brother. If I only knew your name I could introduce him to you, couldn't I?"

Anthony met a frail, blond young man with a minimum of mild chin. Mr. Mills. The girl called Clara took her brother's arm and said: "Come back to the smoking-room when you finish and have a drink. That means you, Mr. Bradell."

"I'd be delighted to come back," Anthony said stiffly, "but I'm afraid it isn't customary for us to drink."

"The custom should be changed," said the dark girl. "But you do dance?

"You don't know my name," she added, fitting herself to him with graceful completeness and precision. "It's Marilee." It would be, Anthony decided, morose. "You have only one name, I suppose," she went on.

The wan warm scent of the brothels of Rio enveloped him. "What would I do with an extra one?" he asked.

Her hair came against his gold epaulet, her lips parted slightly. "Does your sweetheart call you Bradell?" she said. "This music isn't bad, considering what makes it. You'd have quite a nice little boat here if you could only get it to stand straight."

"It takes you there and back," said Anthony.

"You dance divinely, don't you?" she said. "If we only had decent music and a decent floor you'd be marvelous. Am I going to like Buenos Aires?"

"No way of knowing," said Anthony.

"You mean you don't know what I like. That's odd. I feel as though I knew all about you—er—Bradell."

This was more than his painfully developed passenger manner could handle, Anthony admitted, provoked. As to what she liked, if her dancing were any indication, that wouldn't be hard. His mind supplied it, curt, unprintable. He remembered, not without a pleasure in its rigidity, his duty to the passengers. For seeing that this Marilee creature enjoyed her trip so much that Brixton & Heath's competitors didn't get her return passage, he supposed grimly that he was responsible.

In his customary pride of self-control he said: "The name is Anthony."

"Too late," she answered. "I like Bradell better. There! There isn't any more. Thanks loads, Bradell. Let's get a drink."

She detached herself from him with a soft reluctance, sliding an arm through his and turning him aft. "Every one will think I've made a conquest," she said. "Only you and I know how false it is."

At least, Anthony realized, he was being spared perhaps the worst feature of this business, which was having to say something. She was apparently considering his silence, for she asked now: "Have you really a sweetheart somewhere you're afraid you won't be true to? Or do you just hate women? Or are you queer?"

"Just queer," said Anthony briefly.

Her laughter spilled around the corner. "Bradell," she said, "I don't believe it."

"Don't believe what?" he asked, embarrassed.

"Queer." She laughed again.

Anthony went scarlet. "You're pretty loose with your language, aren't you?" he said impotently.

"Awful," she said. "I have to be to make any impression on you, Bradell. How can I help where I lose my heart?" She brought him into the smoking-room, up to a table where the blond girl and Mr. Mills sat drinking. "I expect I'd better get back," Anthony said.

"Sit down, Bradell," said Marilee, "or I'll scream."

She easily might, Anthony decided. On the whole it would be simpler to sit down. She ordered a stinger. "A split of Vichy," Anthony answered Mr. Mills's question.

"I'm glad to see there's no drunkenness among the ship's officers," Marilee said, leaning forward on her elbows. "You aren't drunk, are you, Bradell?"

Miss Mills seemed to think this was funny, but her brother looked thoroughly disapproving. Anthony was astonished to find how disreputable Mr. Mills's absence of chin made disapproval. He couldn't share it as heartily as he wished. "Only speak lower," he said. "Tomorrow the captain will be asking me whether there's so much smoke with no fire."

She, personally, said Marilee, would reassure the captain. Nothing she had ever seen was so proper as Bradell. "By the way," she went on, frowning, "who was that—er—old gentleman in black I saw you with?"

"A friend of the captain's," Anthony answered, startled.

"He's not on board, is he?"

"No. He went ashore."

"That's fine," she said. "I thought I saw him tonight. He gave me the willies. I'm not fooling you, Bradell. I darn near marched ashore. I'll bet I'll see him in my dreams. You don't suppose he was dead, do you?"

"Certainly not," said Anthony, staggered. "His name's Doctor Percival. He—"

"Never mind. I don't want to hear any more," she said sharply. "He ought to be buried. He hasn't any business scaring me to death. Bradell, I don't like to meet corpses walking around. It means something awful is going to happen to me."

"Don't be silly," said Anthony with unconscious directness. "I understood he wasn't well. That's why he looked—"

"Keep still, Bradell," she said, "I know all about that. One more dance and I'll let you go—for tonight. . . ."

He arose and she came and took his arm. Outside she drew him a minute to the rail, gazing down at the lights on the flying water, the dim white crests of the outrushing hull wave. "Looks cool," she said.

"Keep out of it," said Anthony. "It costs us a lot of money to stop."

"I'll keep out," she said. "God, Bradell, I'd hate to drown. No fooling."

Anthony approached the wireless-room again. Couch, the night operator, was just relieving Morris. Morris stepped out on deck. "Hi, Bradell," he said. "Look where you're taking us."

They both glanced up at the thickening sky, starless now. Underfoot, the *San Pedro* was beginning to feel the sea. Her smooth fore-and-aft motion swung off-center deliberately, beginning a roll. From the starboard bow an occasional faint crash of jostled water reached them.

"Better put the cork in," said Morris. "They're going to shake us well before using."

"Maybe not," said Anthony. "We're headed pretty well out. Taken your Mother Sill's?"

"And expected to live," said Morris. "Hold on a minute. Going to see the old man? I got the *San Pablo* again. Maybe he'd like to hear they have nothing to report. Couch," he called, "let's have that last bridge report." He reached through the window. "There you are," he said. "Get it to Garcia."

Anthony went forward. The wind, coming up, made the passage-door hard to open. Inside he paused at the captain's cabin.

"Bradell turning in, sir," he called. "Memorandum on the *San Pablo* under the door. Okay, sir?"

"Step in," came Captain Clendening's voice.

Anthony pushed the door open. The captain was lying on his berth, a magazine in his hands, the reading-light in the corner on. A half-consumed cigar was locked in his teeth. He had got into pajamas and a brilliant silk dressing-gown. Above and behind him, the light cast deep shadows over his eyes. He had his radio on, very quiet, and a low throb of dance-music from New York filled the cigar-hazed air. "Where's the *San Pablo?*" he asked. Anthony handed him the slip. "They ought to be farther along," the captain said fretfully.

"Want them for something, sir?"

"No, no." Captain Clendening threw the magazine aside. "What good are they?"

The cigar had gone out. "Light, sir?" said Anthony, picking up a match-box.

"Never mind, boy," said Captain Clendening. "Smoke too much. Something wrong with my guts."

"Suppose I fix you some bicarb, sir?"

"No good." Captain Clendening ran a hand irritably through the white fur above his ear. "I've got to take care of myself, I guess." He was silent a moment. From New York the foxtrot beat on, smooth and sweet. "Nice music," he said, noticing it. "How's it out?"

"Blowing up, sir."

"I felt it. Where do you suppose we get this list from? Ring up the engine-room and see if we're making any."

Astonished, Anthony took the engine-room telephone.

"Captain wants your bilge soundings," he said. "Ring back. We've got a good load, sir," he continued.

"I guess so," said the captain. "Saw we were wetting our marks."

"Not much, sir," said Anthony, astonished again.

33

"Nothing much. That's the wharfinger's fault. He—"

"Don't you believe that, boy!" roared Captain Clendening. "Don't let me hear you say things like that. You're a sailor, not a steward."

Anthony colored a little. "I meant," he said, "we seem to have to take what we can get, sir."

Captain Clendening jerked his head, twitching his mustache. "Don't feel well," he said more mildly. "You mustn't pay any attention to it. Felt like snapping someone's head off, and you were here, that's all. Great thing to have your youth, boy. You can't keep it, but you ought to think about it sometimes. No point in sleeping through."

The telephone buzzed. Anthony took it up. Turning from it, he said: "They're dry, sir."

"Well, tell them to pump out number two port ballast-tank before morning. Got to straighten us up. God knows what could happen, running into a gale this way."

Anthony returned to the telephone. He must have shown his amazement at concern so exaggerated, for the captain's low left eye winked with a sort of embarrassment. The sagging lump on that side of his chin stood out more. He grunted: "When your insides go back on you it shakes you all up. Just little things. They all get together and you—all of a sudden you see you aren't going to live forever. I'm damned if I know why anyone at sea today wants to live at all, but you do, you do." He bit the dead cigar, the stiff bristles of his mustache brushing it. "You don't like going out, boy. Sort of cold. Sort of lonely. Well, we all got to do it."

The bare blaze of light in the corner, the smoke-filmed air, the harsh photographs of ships—former commands of Captain Clendening's, some lost in the war, some broken up—and especially the captain himself, his hard face puffy in a relaxed brooding, his lumpy form bent a little under the gay silk of the dressing-gown, repeated louder than his words: cold, lonely, old. "They break down," Anthony remembered, "they wear out."

Now, at this bleak moment, the dim contented blare of dance-music fluctuated, feeling the stronger atmospherics. It sagged like a long thread, dipped down, and the mighty ocean covered it in silence. It drew taut again, came fleetingly into earshot, and then it parted. The *San Pedro* drew away in the immense abyss of winds, in the caverns of black water. Only, the *San Pedro* was built for stress; the great turbines turning could never grow tired; the renewed watch above was always sleepless. Men, it seemed to Anthony, were not so well made for living. Energy, power, the vital confidence, grew low as the void grew larger, the ocean mightier and more immense. Eyes wore out with watching; they neither saw nor cared finally—

The *San Pedro* lurched, put her prow hard into rising water, shook from stem to stern. Spray fanned up, curved with the wind and fell in a rippling tap on the starboard ports.

"Took a deep one," said Anthony, rousing himself.

"Turn in, boy," said the captain. "We'll have a wet night."

"Suppose I make a turn around and see that all's secure."

"No. Driscoll did it. Get sleep, boy. Turn in. Forget about it all. May run out by morning."

"Why don't I ask the doctor to step up a minute, sir? He could give you something for your stomach and you'd get a good rest."

"You saw my doctor here this morning," said Captain Clendening. "He knows all about me. He said I ought to be careful. But there wasn't anything to do. I expect I'll rest all right, boy, I'll rest."

THREE

MIRO HAD TO drop his oil-
skins. He caught the hand-rail on the wall, extended
his other hand and found Mr. Bradell's shoulder. He
shook hard. "One bell, sir," he announced. "Thick
weather. Gale from south. Sea high. Temperature, forty-
seven."

Anthony sat up at once, swung his legs out and rubbed
his eyes.

"Wet on the bridge, sir," said Miro. He held onto the
rail. "Let's have a light," Anthony said.

The *San Pedro* with a sort of wanton fury must have
shouldered a hill of water off her bows. She shuddered
distractedly, she seemed to jump up and down. A hundred sharp sounds of her rebelling frame rose in
chorus. Like resolutely planted kicks the throb of her
engines hit her behind. Caught thus between two
hardly resistible forces, the *San Pedro* staggered sideways, the floor tilted, the wall receded. There was a vin-

dictive crash of water, a sort of double jolt as her screws approached the surface.

"Plenty rough," yawned Anthony. He threw a towel into the basin, held on tight and let the water soak it, flung it, one-handed, over his face and head, mopping.

"I got your coffee in a bottle, sir," said Miro.

"Pull out my old uniform, if you can," said Anthony. Water shook from his hair and his face shone. He took the bottle. The coffee he gulped in precarious scalding swallows and it flooded his stomach with a fine hot exhilaration. Bracing himself on the bunk edge, he dressed, putting a sweater on under his uniform coat. "Been like this long?" he asked.

"Not so bad," answered Miro. "It got worse ten, twenty minutes ago. We don't come back very well. Glass gone on the port promenade, a steward told me."

Anthony stamped into his boots, jerked the leather strap at the collar of his slicker and pulled the waterproof hood over his uniform cap. Above, in the warm chart-room, he paused and initialed the night orders. "No change in course," he said.

"It does not seem so, sir," said Miro. He caught Anthony's arm in one hand and the table edge in the other.

"Thanks," said Anthony. They came out.

Mr. Fenton wasn't up yet, but the helmsman had been relieved. Mr. Sheedy, the extra second officer on the mid-watch, grunted with obvious gratitude. "This course is south," he said formally, "fourteen degrees east."

"South fourteen degrees east," Anthony said. He stepped deftly against the roll and came next to the engine-room telegraph.

"Say, this is a rotten blow," said Sheedy. "We're listing plenty. Do you notice?"

"Partly the wind," said Anthony.

"And partly wet water. Why don't you ring up the old man and ask him to let you point off a bit? We get it square in the eye."

"Blow over in a minute, perhaps."

"Carpenter's having a bad time with the port half-door. Can't get it secure, poor devil. Driscoll's up, too, or at least he was, but he didn't call the old man. I hear we broke some glass just now."

Fenton came out, wincing. "God, I cracked my elbow a hot one," he said, stung out of the formalities of bridge etiquette. "What is this, a circus?"

"So long," said Sheedy.

Fenton touched his hidden cap brim.

"I'll step out, Mr. Fenton," Anthony said. "Quartermaster, take a look around starboard." He made his way to the door and let himself onto the open bridge gingerly, moving down the rail almost hand over hand to the shelter at the end. Breathing hard and dripping, he looked forward and the dim radiance of the running light, the glow from the bridge, showed him they were taking it white over the bows every other minute. Fine for those automobiles, he thought. I hope they packed them dry. Growing accustomed to the darkness, he could make out the deck below, and judged that no lines were rigged. It made him wonder what Mr. Driscoll could be doing. He turned and stared aft, but he couldn't see beyond the dim shape of the first life-boat. Something must have happened to the light over the stairs. Bending a little he pulled himself back to the door. Inside he drew off his dripping gloves and went to the telephone.

The minute's long silence broke in his ear with a clean click. "Navigating bridge, sir," he said. "Bradell speaking."

"Well, boy?" came Captain Clendening's voice.

"Permission to change course, sir? Pretty wet forward."

"Do what you want. Shall I come up?"

"No, sir. Nothing wrong."

"Half-speed, Mr. Fenton," Anthony said. "Half-speed, sir," said Mr. Fenton, snapping over the telegraph.

"Helm!" said Anthony. The helmsman glanced over his shoulder, stood aside, fastening both hands on one spoke. Anthony stepped in and took it. He drew the wheel right, hand over hand. The electric telltale went to half rudder.

"Port full ahead, Mr. Fenton!"

"Port full ahead, sir."

The *San Pedro* gained steerageway, came staggering over. She buried her starboard bow and the white water thundered down. She tilted up and rode the next one. "Two-thirds, Mr. Fenton."

The telltale went amidships. Anthony bent his face into the binnacle light. "The course is due south," he said. "Look alive! Nothing off."

The helmsman stood on.

"Well," said Mr. Fenton, "I guess the worst is over."

At six o'clock, dawn, delayed, was pale on the forecastle. Miro relieved the helmsman. Anthony had attempted full ahead twice, but they made wet work of it. Captain Clendening, up to the ears in his bridge coat, appeared now. He returned the salute of the watch incompletely, holding onto a window and staring out forward. He stood so long, swaying loosely with the movement of the ship, that even Miro at the helm began to watch him, apprehensive.

"What are we doing, Mr. Bradell?" he said at last. "About two knots?"

"About five, sir, I think."

"List is worse," he said. He came and stared at the clinometer. "Anything shifted yet?"

"Not that I know of, sir."

"Where's Mr. Driscoll?"

"I think he's still below, sir, at the half-door. They were making quite a lot of water."

"I want to see him. Look up the chief officer, Mr. Fenton."

His face in the strengthening light was so haggard that Anthony said: "Take some coffee, sir. The vacuum bottle's full in the chart-room."

"Don't want it now," he answered. "Turn out the morning watch, Mr. Bradell. I want to heave to and find out what's wrong with us. What do we need for steerageway?"

"I guess one-third, sir."

"All right. Helm! Mind your rudder. Get on, Mr. Bradell."

Anthony supposed it was ten o'clock when the fore-and-aft bulkhead in upper hold number one stove. Two cased automobiles shifted fifteen feet to port, knocking down the wall of the port bunk-room. The wedges probably came loose when they had lain-to while wind and sea on their port quarter shook them so heavily. That helpless half-hour had been a little worse than futile, then. He went forward with Mr. Eberly. The junior second officer said: "Well, maybe the old man will feel better now. We got something wrong here all right."

Anthony understood Mr. Eberly's attitude but he understood, too, Captain Clendening's earlier exasperation at their failure to find anything which would account for the list. He said nothing now, viewing the bunk-room attentively. In the working alleyway there was water over his ankles. At the half-door Mr. Driscoll was still busy in a grim, conscientious silence. He had several seamen with him and they were trying to tighten the dogs with a persistence which had become, considering the simplicity of the task, merely maddening. Anthony had an impatient desire to get at that job himself and finish it up. It was too senseless. They had been working there off and on for eight hours without effecting a change. To avoid any such officiousness he turned back to Mr. Eberly and said: "We'd gone over pretty far to make them slide. This sea will have to go down before we can do much. I don't believe they'll move again."

"Say, listen, white man," rose a querulous voice from the firemen's forecastle beyond, "how we sleep?"

"Pipe down!" called Anthony sharply.

"We got water, mister."

He went up the passage. "Oh," he said, "you have a port out."

The bunk-room was running underfoot. Two electric bulbs burned and sickly morning light came with the recurring splashes of water through the broken port. A strong smell arose; wet wool and bedding, old sweat. Wrapped in blankets, like lively mummies on shelves, forms stirred, white eyeballs rolled in the shadows. The crazy man, Quail, caught the iron bunk post above, swung himself out and down with one arm, like a chimpanzee. He landed squatly on his feet in the shallow water. "I want to be home," he moaned. He beat his great swinging fist on his chest; his voice rolled and boomed from the depths. "I got those home-again blues." His conical skull swayed from side to side. "Home," he chanted, "knock on the door!"

"Lay off, nigger," snapped Anthony. "I'll have the carpenter in."

"Quail, he think he swim. Long way New York, Quail." Laughter exploded richly in the bunks.

"Quail, he feel water, he fear soap to come!"

Quail held onto the post. "Home, just as before," he moaned. "Home again, to roam no more. . . ."

Most of the late morning Mr. MacGillivray had a crew on the ash-ejector valve. It must have worked loose during the heavy weather while they were heaved-to earlier. By noon they had it tight again, but water was pouring smoothly into the stoke-hole by the bunker chutes. It slopped around the dog box and washed back and forth on the plates. Perhaps a bunker-hatch cover

43

had gone and Mr. MacGillivray suggested this to the bridge. He did not know whether they had done anything about it or not but he had started a pump at half past ten and still needed it. In fact he would have used all his pumps but he had been ordered to empty the rest of the port ballast-tanks. Meanwhile he was clearing his bilge by not more than a foot an hour and the whole place was in a mess, with pressure falling off. It was useless to tell the fire-room to shake her up. The men worked resentfully with a psychological slowness in a flooded stoke-hole. Mr. MacGillivray wished often and audibly to God that they were on oil, independent of firemen with wet feet and trimmers who were constantly losing their rakes in the shallow water.

It was his only public concession to the annoyances of the situation, which were, to his mind, many. Among other things, he wouldn't get to luncheon and he had a nice crowd at his table, including two good-looking women who called him chief and knew a funny story when they heard one—well, that was the way it always worked, and probably they were seasick anyway. There would be plenty more meals when they got South and had nicer weather. At the moment it was still remarkably rough. Much rougher than there was any need for it to be, he decided, having gone above a moment for the purpose. Most of it was the half-witted way they handled the ship.

Half past three, declared the clock on the stairs which Anthony had just passed, moving down the port alleyway of the C deck. He was going aft to find out what had

44

been done five minutes before by a green sea taken broad on the quarter. It pooped them with a shock like a hill falling aboard. Anthony could not figure it out— how, in view of wind, weather, and the *San Pedro*'s course, it ever got there. He was extraordinarily tired. In this state, the ocean became almost personified; a purposeful and malicious agent, driving its heavy assaults to the unexpected and unguarded points. At the *San Pedro*'s heavy stagger, Captain Clendening went out and looked aft. Obviously a boat had gone from the steerage superstructure, for one thing. The supports of the after-bridge were twisted. White water cascaded endlessly off the poop-deck as the fantail shook itself free. You could hear the descending crash all the way forward. He said without emphasis: "Find out what carried away, Mr. Bradell."

Anthony went, as smartly as he could make his aching legs move. He was certain that it would prove to have been particularly, wantonly, destructive. The steerage passengers were probably in a panic. In fact, there was no reason to suppose they hadn't lost a few people overboard. Anthony reviewed these possibilities in a stupor of resentment. A figure was approaching him in the alleyway and he faltered a moment, trying to calculate by the lethargic lurch of the tilted floor whether to pass right or left.

"Hello, Bradell," she said. "Such a nice day, isn't it?"

She moved a little with the shift underfoot, and managed, intentionally or not, to block the whole alleyway, so he had to halt. "Sorry," he said. "I've got to get aft."

"Listen, Bradell," she said. "Do something about this.

45

Clara and tons of people are sick as dogs. And I can't even get a bath. The bath-steward says we aren't level enough. I'll be positively filthy if it keeps up many weeks." She regarded him with clear good humor and he saw that her eyes were blue. "You don't look well, Bradell," she continued critically. "Have a sleepless night? So did I. I couldn't get my mind off you. And the food is atrocious, such of it as stays on the table. It was bad enough before."

"Sorry," repeated Anthony. "Don't worry. Everything is all right."

All the woodwork creaked and cried out with the roll. She put a hand on his arm and said: "Good Lord, is it as bad as that?"

She seemed obscurely to cling to him, impeding his thought as well as his progress. He felt too tired to shake her off, so he said: "No danger at all. Everything is all right."

"Listen, Bradell," she said. "Tell me how bad it is. I'll be simply furious if I find out afterward we almost sank and I didn't even know it. A girl has to have some kick out of life."

"Everything is all right," said Anthony, looking at her.

She frowned a little, tightening the fingers on his arm.

"I thought at first there couldn't be anything wrong," she said, "because so many of the passengers were scared. Listen, Bradell, why don't you say it's the worst storm you've seen in ninety-seven years at sea, or something?"

"No danger," he said. "I've got to get aft."

"Bradell," she said, "you don't hate me enough to go and drown all these innocent people, too, do you? Besides, I told you I damn well didn't want to drown."

"All right," he exploded wearily. "You won't. Don't be such a fool."

Her face was getting whiter and whiter under the rouge. "Listen," she said, somewhat more huskily. "I've got plenty of nerve, but you have to tell me one thing." She hesitated an instant. "Bradell, are you sure that doctor man went ashore?"

"I've got to get aft," said Anthony, "I can't talk to you."

"Bradell, you weren't fooling me?"

"I can't talk to you," said Anthony. "Please step aside."

She moved, backing against the white-paneled wall, extending a lax arm on either side of her to grasp the hand-rail. She murmured: "Good-by, Bradell."

He passed her. Although he did not look, he could feel her still there, her dark head up, leaning against the wall mutely, her blue eyes on his retreating back.

In the wireless-room Smith, the first operator, regarded Morris without favor. Morris was on duty. He had, as usual, the phones pushed off one ear. A cigarette nodded up and down as he hummed to himself. His tobacco-dyed forefinger kept the key in a vibrating, whining chatter—QSU—QRN—QRU. . . . The *San Pedro*'s WPRV went on to the end. He locked his hands in back of his head and sucked at the cigarette.

"Who was that?" asked Smith, still sleepy.

"San Pablo."

"We aren't reporting anything?"

"Having a fine time. Wish you were here. Want me to write a poem, or tell 'em the one about the stuffed monkeys?"

"It doesn't feel so good to me," said Smith. "Where did we get all this water?"

"Elephant charged the camera," said Morris, delighted, "but I dropped him at twenty paces. He's in the wastepaper basket."

"Funny boy, aren't you?" said Smith. "Are we all right?"

"As advertised," said Morris. He drawled with relish, gleeful: "These magnificent vessels are unsurpassed in comfort and luxury. Having been especially constructed for tropical voyaging, the ventilation of every room is perfect—just feel it," he said, turning up his collar. "Running water, too," he added, "in every room now. Some with baths."

"Don't, I'll die!" said Smith.

"Appetizing meals to delight the keen appetites aroused by the bracing sea air—" He seized a partly consumed ham sandwich from the plate beside him. "Do take some more caviar, count," he said. "It will only be thrown out."

"Say, listen," said Smith. "Is that all we get to eat?"

"That? You don't even get that. That's mine. Try and find another. While you were absent they procured five tons of sea water somewhere at great expense and put them in the ranges. Didn't they consult you?"

48

"After the applause dies down, let's see the bridge orders."

"Help yourself," said Morris cordially. "The old man keeps wanting to know where the *San Pablo* is, as if I gave a damn! When I get them, he doesn't want them for anything. Their lad told me for God's sake to leave them alone. That shows how little he's been out. Nothing like a valve transmitter in unscrupulous hands, I always say. We'll bother them, if you want to know, from thirty-five to forty-five on twenty-one hundred continuous every hour for the rest of the night."

"What's the idea?"

"Oh, just a little thing I tossed off while I was waiting. It isn't finished yet, of course, but the old man certainly liked it."

"Listen, I'll relieve you now. Like a good sport, go down and get me a sandwich, will you?"

"Wrong," protested Morris.

"Listen, have I got to order you?"

"No, no, don't feel that way. Accidents happen."

"Go on, get up. You got a drag down there."

"Say, you certainly presume on your white hairs, Lord Algy," groaned Morris. "All together now; American Marconi Company, I love you!"

The narrow promenade around the fantail had lost a long section of rail. On the port side the Third-Class pantry had been flushed out clean. The door was carried away; every detachable object was swept through with the rail. For the moment it would be simpler to

49

assume that no one had been on duty there, Anthony decided. He continued around the stern. Not a square inch of glass was left in any exposed window. The stewards would have to rope off the unprotected deck, and looking for them, he put his shoulder against the starboard entry doors.

Inside, the constricted stairs came up to the Third-Class lounge. Furniture consisted mainly of benches fastened to the walls, but there was a big table. This had torn out the pin of the stay-chain, overturning and scattering newspapers and old magazines on the linoleum, shining with dirty water. Forty faces, black or palely Negroid, lifted to Anthony. The high, miserable storm of voices quailed a moment. Then the sight of his uniform cap drove up a louder wail; partly hysterical relief at finding they were not alone in the world, partly fresh panic at the appearance of authority, in most of their minds associated with disaster and unreasonable suffering to come.

Anthony endeavored to ignore them, but his rapid and accurate eye included them all. Some sat paralyzed, bundles of their poor possessions done up in sheets resting at their feet. Others had gotten inefficiently into lifebelts. One group appeared to be praying, led by a monstrous woman with a mustache. More practical, another group had procured several bottles.

"Steward!" Anthony called.

Not understanding him, most of them joined in, too; a general lamentation. The old woman with the mustache shrieked louder. The people with bundles laid hold of them. A man with a bottle tilted it up as far as it would go.

"Pipe down!" shouted Anthony. "Shut up! You're all right." He realized that they did not understand him. "No hay periculo! Basta! Basta!"

That exhausted his Spanish, but they understood at least that he was trying to talk to them. With appalling suddenness a silence fell, marred on the edges by stifled groans and sobs. They swayed visibly toward him, all eyes fastened to him, all waiting for him to perform some miracle and save them.

"No hay periculo," repeated Anthony. "Esta bien."

His broken Spanish was worse than nothing. It frightened them more. The uncertainty of his accent, the inadequacy of his words, made everything he said improbable, sinister even. They were clearly cut off from the people who had them in charge, who had brought them to this extremity and alone could deliver them. The moaning swelled up again and Anthony shouted: "Doesn't anyone speak English?"

Livid under his black skin one man said nervelessly: "What you like to say, señor?"

"Tell them to go back to their staterooms."

"No, no, mister," he wailed. "No, no. Room full of water. People sick. People scared. No, no."

"Tell them."

"No, no," he groaned. "Ship sink. People drown. Leave those here, mister."

"Where's the steward?"

"What you say, mister?"

"The steward!"

51

"No, no, mister. No, no."

"Where is the man with the white coat?" Anthony shouted.

"Some gone. Some sick in room. Some under bed."

"Where?" said Anthony. "Show me."

"No, no. I stay here, mister. No, no."

Anthony did not move, but simple savagery must have shown in his face, for the man cowered away into the corner, backing against people who parted struggling to keep far from Anthony. Their shrieks swelled up again. The whole frail fabric of human relationships melted now in a mess of paralyzed muscle and brain and will. More shocking than the most murderous resistance, they became simply dead weight. They were lumps weighing some hundred and fifty pounds, too yielding to grasp, too misshapen to handle. Anthony stood dark-eyed and stiff-faced. He wanted to plant his feet in these quivering gelatinous heaps. He was shaken to the bottom—indeed there was no bottom, only the unthinkable abyss of human impotence opened under him. His brain, suspended over it, counseled him merely to kill, trample them down, destroy them, before their shocking contagion destroyed him. The blood beat up and filmed over his eyes, and he was saved by a quick, idiotic irrelevancy. He recognized that he was seeing red; that there was such a thing, no figure of speech, but a bloody mist. The childish surprise of it unsprung his nerves. He turned stiffly, grasped the rail of the stairs, and, putting one foot before another, descended. At the bottom his voice came like a croak, but he cleared it and shouted: "Steward!"

52

A figure appeared uncertainly at the end of the little passage. "Where are the others?" Anthony asked.

"In the pantry, they were," faltered this man, glassy-eyed.

Three, maybe four, men gone, swept off and smothered somewhere in the broken wake, was a fact, literal and sharp. At once the misery of wetness and fear, the noise above, like animals crowded in a dangerous pen, became a simpler thing, pitiable. If, a moment ago, Anthony could have wished them all scoured out by the hard sea, buried away and obliterated, now he felt only their wretched humanity, their common helplessness against the inhuman ocean.

"Poor devils," he murmured. The man's enormous eyes looked up at him. "All right," Anthony said. "We can't do anything now. Buck up!"

The man opened his mouth and no sound came out, but finally he said: "Yes, sir."

"Unlock the passage-door there. I'll get some men down to you. Everything is all right. Go above and don't let anyone out. Half the rail's carried away."

"Yes, sir." The steward spoke more securely. He at least had the outlines of a discipline, however irregular or casual. This framework propped him up a little, made him firm enough to grasp. Once grasped, the current of command galvanized him. His chin rose, his shaking ceased. "Yes, sir," he repeated quickly.

"Look alive," said Anthony. "We'll probably be out of this before dark."

*

At nine o'clock Mr. MacGillivray and his fourth engineer finished work on the extra pump. Designed for blowing ashes or supplying water to the deck fire-lines, they turned it on the stubbornly making bilge, broke the joint connection and fitted on a screen filter. That raised their available horse-power to about two hundred. As there was never anything wrong with the gear in an engine-room ruled by Mr. MacGillivray, the pumps were better than seventy per cent efficient. Together they sucked up a ton of water a minute, heaved it thirty feet from the level of the fire-room plates, and dumped it over the side.

The chief viewed this arrangement, satisfied. He did not know where so much water could be coming from, but he was, he felt sure, more than a match for it. He would have his bilges dry before morning. If it came to that, he could and would pump out the whole blasted ocean. He'd have no dirty water in his department.

Presently he went above to clean up. Soaping his big hands, he felt rather grumpy. As he got older he tended more and more to regard sailors, deck officers, as a not very necessary nuisance. If they ever developed a tenth of the efficiency he demanded and received from his personnel, from his main plant, from every fitting and auxiliary, there might be some sense in shipping. As it was, you took the finest turbines made by man and put them in a tin scow run by a lot of damn fools who filled it with water, ran it on its side and near shook the lagging off. He was tired now, but he certainly wasn't turning in until they got a grip on things. Though the sea was moderating, the *San Pedro* rolled heavily. The list was to twenty degrees and he didn't believe what water he had was doing it.

Returning to his office, he put on his uniform coat and settled at the desk, his hands folded on his belly, his porcelain-blue eyes brooding. He was there when the alleyway door opened and he saw that at last the captain had come below. Mr. MacGillivray got to his feet. Mr. Bradell had entered with the old man. He stood at his elbow, as though he were helping him to walk, and the chief noticed that Captain Clendening moved heavily, without determination.

"Evening, captain," he said shortly.

"How is it?" said Captain Clendening at last.

"We're all right," Mr. MacGillivray said. "Got three pumps on. Have us dry pretty soon. Can't we do something about this list? Throws my lubrication off. Burn out a bearing somewhere, I wouldn't be surprised." Actually he would be stunned with surprise. He had an extraordinary extra-sense for developing friction; it would be a clever bearing that burnt out in his engine-room.

"Where do you think the water's coming from, Mac-Gillivray?" Captain Clendening asked.

Mr. MacGillivray pulled his loose chin. "It's black water," he said. "Must come through the coal. Don't suppose we sprung a plate?"

"I don't know," said Captain Clendening.

Mr. MacGillivray looked at him sharply. "Aren't you trying to find out?" he asked.

"Since about four this morning," interposed Mr. Bradell, "we haven't done anything else, chief."

55

"Now, if I were you, son," said Mr. MacGillivray, "I'd get myself in overalls and poke about the port bunkers. You can get in from the shelter-deck. Take an electric flashlight and keep it dry—"

"I'll give Bradell his orders, Mr. MacGillivray," said Captain Clendening.

"Just offering a suggestion," said Mr. MacGillivray, his mouth pouting out from the hanging folds of cheek. "Seems to me about time something was done."

Captain Clendening's lumpy jaw sagged down and forward. His mustache stiffened. "By God, sir," he roared, "I'll have you understand, Mr. MacGillivray, that I am in command of this ship. When I want your suggestions, I'll ask for them!"

"Very good," said Mr. MacGillivray. "And now I'll step below, with your permission, and get on with more important matters."

He turned his back on them. The clear snorts of his breathing sounded above the roar of the engine-room shaft for a moment. He stumped down the steel steps.

Captain Clendening swallowed audibly. "Boy?" he said.

"Yes, sir," said Anthony.

Captain Clendening made an uneasy gesture. "Go down, boy," he said. "My apologies to Mr. MacGillivray. Sort of nervous, boy. Guts are no good. Got to take care of myself. Tell him I appreciate his hard work. Tell him I rely on him absolutely and I hope he'll see fit to overlook my—my"—he faltered—"my language, that is."

"Yes, sir," said Anthony. The captain's mouth worked

a little and Anthony hesitated, not knowing if he were finished.

The captain's eyes came back to him, focussed harder a moment. "Mr. Bradell!"

"Yes, sir."

"Perhaps you can tell me who is in command of this vessel?"

"You are, sir," said Anthony, dumfounded.

"Thank you. When I give an order, I want it obeyed. What are you standing here for? Look alive, sir! I'll have no oil-tanker customs on this ship!"

FOUR

MIRO HAD GONE below when Mr. Bradell told him to turn in. Wind, weather; noise, no matter how relentless; discomfort very severe, he could ignore when he was ready to sleep. Now, long past midnight, he knew no such thing had disturbed him. His eyes open in the dark, he was at once alert, roused from within. Believing that an angel watched over him, he recognized instantly what had happened. This invisible being, who saw all and knew all, had bent down suddenly. The tall shadow fell on him, the great wings fanned him.

He was not perturbed, nor was he hurried, though it could mean only that danger had become at last real and imminent. Perhaps all day danger had been mounting, like fluid in a pressure tube. Now it had crossed a mark and its crossing touched off tremendous alarms. His inquiring physical senses assured him that to every appearance nothing had changed. Slow and steady, the hammer of the engines at half-speed and time continued; the *San Pedro* rolled sluggishly; water forward bumped and crashed. A sound of movement and still calm enough voices came from the working alleyway. All the greater reason to find out, if he could, what subtler or more sinister change had caught his angel's sleepless eye.

He had not taken off his boots, so he came at once to his feet. The occasional lights of the narrow wet passage, tilted badly by the list, burned dim in their heavy cups of misted glass. He proceeded aft to the working alleyway and saw to his astonishment a dozen men from the steward's department. The half-door, he observed immediately, had carried away altogether. The carpenter was there, trying to rig a new one of boards and canvas. It was not completed and only partly in place, so when they leaned far on the list the sea came right in. One had a momentary staggering glimpse of their dull lights spilling into the void, winking on fathomless black swells almost under foot. Coming back enough to conceal this ugly phenomenon, the water already shipped surged to starboard like a miniature tidal wave. It went above the knees of the carpenter and his mate, busy with their boards.

Mr. Driscoll had been absent a moment before, but Miro saw him now, buttoned up in his bridge coat, his face remarkably white in the bad light. He picked out Miro in the shadow beyond and said: "Quartermaster?"

Miro answered, greatly relieved to find the chief officer in such alert charge.

"See if you can rout out some more men here. Get a

lot of men. Any men you can." Mr. Driscoll supported himself with one hand on the clammy wall as the *San Pedro* went over and the half-door framed the black sea like a steep floor. "Wait," he said.

"Yes, sir."

"Report to the bridge first. Tell the captain that the situation doesn't seem to improve. You might ask if it would be possible for him to step below here a moment. I—er—" He became conscious of the deadly silence of the men listening. "Hurry up," he jerked out. "Get on with it."

Mr. Driscoll, then, was worried, too. Miro, in point of private fact, had small respect for Mr. Driscoll as a seaman. He did not believe now that Mr. Driscoll knew what ought to be done, nor even how to go about whatever substitute for the right thing he might have in mind. Mounting the inside stairs to the chart-room, Miro decided to report to Mr. Bradell first. Mr. Bradell could tell him what to do, and once sure himself, he might discover some way to modify Mr. Driscoll's designs.

He found this intention defeated, however. He appeared quietly in the door, and was dismayed to see the wheel-house almost crowded. Both Mr. Eberly and Mr. Sheedy were standing by. Young Mr. Fenton and the third officer were close together in the corner. The fifth officer, Mr. Eberly's junior, balanced himself restlessly with the roll, looking at the ceiling. Mr. Bradell, his arms folded tight, the brim of his cap down over his forehead, stood beside the engine-room telegraph. The helmsman's eyes swung furtively from the binnacle to the rudder indicator and then sideways, as though appealing to Mr. Bradell.

Unnoticed in the door behind, Miro considered them one after another. They were all tired, yet they were all alert, too, quiet and composed, but obviously mystified. One could deduce that they were here because they had been ordered up. They had not been told why, they had not been told what to do. No one spoke; they simply waited. It was, in its inept, mute, rather bewildered way, magnificent, and Miro appreciated this. Here was a very superior form of *tela*, a splendid, passive morale, the supreme ability to remain motionless and to appear calm; to stand endlessly ready for no one knew what.

Since Mr. Bradell had the watch, it would be impossible to speak to him. Miro hesitated soundlessly, considering to whom he should speak. At this moment the port door onto the open bridge moved and Captain Clendening came in.

His face under the electric light was positively lifeless, but it had a surface shine from the spray on it. His eyes were so far swollen that they seemed to wink craftily out of slits. He stood heavy and clumsy in his wet bridge coat a moment. All glances had gone to him, but they wavered now, went away. There was a slight simultaneous movement of lips and eyes returning to careful impassivity. Mr. Bradell never budged, had not looked.

Paying no attention to his waiting officers, Captain Clendening kept his face toward Miro. "Yes?" he said.

"Chief officer reports, sir," said Miro. "Mr. Driscoll wants to know if you can step below, sir."

There was a general restrained stir, but no other sound.

"No," said Captain Clendening. "Tell him to carry on."

The helmsman let his brown, nervous face turn. "Helm!" said Mr. Bradell. The helmsman's eyes jerked front.

In his gray-yellow face Captain Clendening's eyeballs flickered. A slight muscular contraction shook the thick cheeks. "Turn in, Mr. Eberly," he said. "Get some sleep. Won't want you after all." He jerked his head toward the third and fifth officers. "You, too," he said. "Turn in. Mr. Sheedy, report to the chief officer."

They all moved immediately in the grateful release of definite orders.

"Quartermaster?"

"Yes, sir."

"Find out from the wireless-room where the *San Pablo* is."

"Yes, sir."

"Mr. Bradell?"

"Yes, sir."

"Can you carry on a little longer?"

"Yes, sir."

Miro was out through the chart-room. In his ears repeated and repeated the mechanical "Yes, sir," "Yes, sir." It lost all alacrity, all smart and competent obedience. The phrase hammered and hammered. Under the senseless impact, the framework of observation— the vital initiative, the intelligence to see clearly and do quickly—cracked, crumbled to dust. Discipline, directed coöperation, ceased here to have any virtue. Habit betrayed the will and debauched the brain. Physically, the lips might stiffen with reluctance, the voice almost fail, but the mind in its extremity knew only one reply. To disaster, to stupid folly, to terrible peril which might yet be averted or resisted; to the advance of death itself, the mind acquiescent, drugged with a phrase, answered only, "Yes, sir."

Wet wind hit Miro in the face. Beneath his feet the deck tilted away. He caught a hand-rail; he saw the dim bands of the *San Pedro*'s funnel stagger in the dark. He knew now that the *San Pedro* was certainly foundering, however slowly, and that most of those she carried might be lost.

Tuckerton, New Jersey. East Moriches, Long Island. All night rain has fallen on the Atlantic coast. Dawn is up, wet from the eastern ocean, but before six o'clock the sullen skies were breaking. Heavy smell of wet trees, wide wet meadows, and the warm damp earth spread everywhere; through country streets, silent, but brighter; into the quiet open windows of houses still asleep. There followed presently a thin noise of bird song. Over the edge of the world, just about level with the drenched tree-tops, poured out the sun. Its flat, enormous shafts struck resplendent across the Eastern States. At Tuckerton, and at East Moriches, far higher than trees, slender and rigid against the fine dissolving blue, stood up the skeleton towers of the coastal wireless stations.

Under them, in the power-houses, in the offices and

operating rooms, some of the lights were turned off. Shifts of operators and engineers changed. The great generators, not requiring relief, spun on, subdued; but there was a sound of released voices on the beautiful air outside. An early train had tossed off the New York papers, and men walking slowly home to bed lit cigarettes, looked at them, and saw there was no news worth reading.

Inside, the morning reliefs were settling down. Outside, soundless, invisible, humanly indetectable, the serene, the golden June air swelled, grew full with rising volume; the racing, screaming whine of code communication; broadcasting voices clearly relayed; early music.

At seven-fifteen, into these crowded currents which carried the immense record of the awakened world, cut faintly the *San Pedro*'s CQ—a thin plea, staccato with foreboding. From far off the Virginia Capes they were nagging at human attention; *everybody listen*. At Tuckerton, at East Moriches, the emergency operators stirred, attentive, mildly curious, as a half-hour silence settled. Just before eight o'clock came the SOS. By eight o'clock the Brooklyn Navy Yard was suspending all radio traffic. Over the whole of Eastern North America the air was abruptly emptied and into this immense void the *San Pedro* called again, small and solitary; faded out; called once more, appealing now to the Naval Compass Station at Cape May for her true bearings.

They heard it on the largest ship in the world; the white vessels of the United Fruit Company, many-decked Clyde liners, a dozen ships of the Caribbean and Southern trade, picked it up, calculating the scores of separating miles. Slow, dogged, steaming stockily, the Japanese freighter *Toledo Maru* halted a hundred miles away and came heavily about; from the North Atlantic steamship lanes a moderately fast Cunarder broke, turned south, forcing her draft; a German boat, farther east, bound for New York, turned, too. Just over the horizon a small sugar tramp from Cuba came abreast, passed the *San Pedro*, crawled patiently on, not being equipped with wireless.

Captain Clendening's eyeballs were finely netted with scarlet veins. There was a silver stubble of beard over his square cheeks. Beneath his short white mustache his mouth opened and shut, sucking in the cool air. He held onto the shutter of the open wheel-house window, and the cumbersome seas, whipping up the tilted well-deck forward, staggering into the port half-doors, were gray with advanced morning. The *San Pedro*, resisting them, shook him back and forth on his feet, but he held on. He held the tighter, for he did not wish to turn around; he felt, insistent, the need to look back, to survey the boat-deck again, but he put it off a moment while his head wabbled. "Got to take care of myself," he murmured, for he knew that he was very sick, ought to be in bed. In answer he held himself still tighter, harder, while he did turn and look back. He realized then that he could not see anything unless he went out on the open bridge end. There was, however, a quartermaster gazing at him. The man's eyes were dark, sad, deep as wells. "Order to abandon, sir?" he said softly.

Captain Clendening was stunned. He opened his

mouth to roar, but his throat failed him. He could not believe that he had understood; that on his own bridge a quartermaster could be offering him a suggestion. He breathed harder, he held tighter, as though he were climbing a vertical slope. The situation was so outrageous and amazing that, still speechless, he wondered if it might not have been his imagination, for the man was saying normally, like any quartermaster: "Chief officer reports starboard boats impractical, sir."

He hesitated and Captain Clendening, his mouth tight, his eyes hard ahead, continued to look at him.

"Mr. Bradell asked me to say, sir, that port boats could be dropped in the lee and get off. May he reverse orders, sir?"

Captain Clendening studied him, studied his brown clear skin and melancholy liquid eyes, knew that he had noticed him often before, that this was a reliable man. "What's your name?" he asked.

"Miro, sir," answered the quartermaster. There was a sudden brightening of his eyes as though he were about to weep.

They were all inordinately sensitive, these Southerners; particularly, intelligent ones; Captain Clendening knew. He modified his tone a little. "Don't you know how to behave on the bridge, boy?" he said. "Look alive and speak when you're spoken to."

"Yes, sir," said Miro.

"Well, what did you want?"

"About life-boat stations, sir. Mr. Bradell—"

"I gave no orders about boats," said Captain Clendening, his voice thick in his ears. "What are you talking about?"

The man's deep sad eyes with the far-away glint of tears stayed on him steadily. "You will remember, sir," he said. His voice was mild, very gentle, but distinct. "You ordered Mr. Bradell and Mr. Driscoll to turn to on the boats."

"I sent Mr. Bradell forward," said Captain Clendening. "What's he doing with the boats?"

"Yes, sir," said the soft clear voice. "That was afterward. He has gone forward now, sir."

"Why didn't you report at once? I'll have no tampering with—"

He found, to his amazement, that he must have been interrupted. "I try to report, sir, for ten, twenty minutes. I have been right here, sir. I do not think that you have heard me." The man's face was a still, tragic mask with the small deep pools of the eyes. "Boats have broken on the side, sir. It is too—"

"Officers," said Captain Clendening, "will carry out their orders to the best of their ability." He extended a hand. "I want to go onto the bridge," he said.

Miro came close, more like a sudden close-up in a motion-picture than ordinary movement. Miro's hard, neatly muscled shoulder steadied Captain Clendening. Very sure-footed, Miro calculated the movement of the ship, moving with it, and they were out, under the terrible white light of the pale sky. Captain Clendening shook off Miro's support, holding the rail and watching the concerted movement about the life-boats. His

67

mouth was full of spittle, tasting brazen, or bitter, and he swallowed steadily, trying to get rid of it.

Now someone else had appeared at the wheel-house door. Captain Clendening tightened his jaw and said: "You have your orders, Mr. Fenton. Be good enough to carry them out." The quartermaster was still gazing at him, so he added, enraged at last by the implacable sadness of the eyes: "Get that man out of here, Mr. Fenton. I'll have him in irons if he leaves his post again."

He heard Mr. Fenton's voice: ". . . get some of them away, sir?" and it occurred to him that he might not have spoken aloud in reference to the quartermaster. He saw no use in repeating it. To Mr. Fenton he said automatically: "You will await an order for general abandonment. How are the passengers?"

"Mr. Eberly and Mr. Sheedy are in charge, sir. Women and children mustered up. All behaving well."

"Right," said Captain Clendening. "We'll have no *La Bourgogne* business here."

Still a third man had appeared. He recognized this one as from the wireless-room. He had in his hand several papers. His voice awoke in an animated drawl. "Yes, yes," said Captain Clendening sharply. He did not want to listen to this, so he took the scribbled reports from the young man. "Carry on," he said, anxious to get rid of them.

In the wireless-room Smith was at the key. "On the coil now," he said to Morris, returning. "When are we going to abandon?"

Morris lit a cigarette, propped himself in the tilted

68

corner. He employed his free hand thoughtfully, scratching his red hair. "Nobody knows," he hummed, "and nobody seems to care."

"Listen," said Smith. "Don't wisecrack. I don't mind telling you I want to live. How's the old man?"

"He's all right," said Morris. He hesitated an instant, examining the palms of his hands. Then he wiped them deliberately on the seams of his uniform trousers. "He looks pretty bad. You don't lose your ship every day, now I come to think of it, but he's playing ball."

"What's he say?"

"Nothing," answered Morris. "Which seems to me to be about right. They stove in another boat just now." His face stirred, became lively, grinning. "Pretty soon we'll have to take off our shoes and stockings and wade; that is, those not otherwise engaged. I'll flip you to see who does the Casabianca stunt. We'll count Couch out, since he wouldn't be on duty anyway. Where is he, having a quiet nap?"

"Out with Mr. Driscoll. He's had some experience with boats."

"If he has, he's the only one," said Morris. "I could tell you a good joke, only it might upset you. Let's have a half-dollar."

"I'll stay," said Smith. "I'm the senior operator."

"You're sure hell on heroism," said Morris, enlivened, "but I've only one cigarette left, so I might as well drown. Furthermore, what did I happen to find but a quart of Bacardi, which will take away the taste of salt water something wonderful. I'll even give you a drink if you'll lend me your boy-scout knife."

"Now, shut up!" said Smith sharply. "Don't get all worked up. Everything's all right. We'll float for eight hours at least and by three o'clock—"

"You must have heard Mr. Eberly talking to the passengers," said Morris. "That's the good joke. I was going to tell you. He has them all down on the promenade-deck, and since they don't know him very well— some of them have barely met him—they think he knows what it's all about."

"And I suppose you know a hell of a lot more?"

"I know this," said Morris modestly. "If we don't stop leaning over the rail, we're going to capsize. Thank God I'm not a seaman; I'd miss all the fun of expecting it."

"You aren't so damn humorous," said Smith.

"Get off the key," said Morris, "and let me hand these boys a few sad brave remarks."

"Don't be an ass!" said Smith. "What juice we have we'll keep. Hang on, I got the Jap boat again."

He penciled down letters in silence. "You didn't bring back any new bearings, did you?" he asked Morris over his shoulder. "They've got a ten-cent outfit with no direction finder."

"Shoot them something snappy for a come-on," said Morris. "Don't be a Western Union messenger all your life."

"Shut up," said Smith. His key awoke, and Morris, reading it off, translated freely: " 'Bad enough here old man position ship in hardly stay receive please hurry—' That's right," he said. "Probably they were wondering about that last part. Probably they didn't know whether to hurry or to stop and do a little fishing."

"For God's sake, shut up!" shouted Smith.

"Sorry," said Morris. "Didn't mean to spoil our last happy hours together. Well, before we get any more good news, I'll flip you two out of three for that space on the Memorial in Battery Park, the bottle, and all your cigarettes. Come on, boy, think of your lovin' wife."

Smith said glumly: "Well, at any rate I haven't got that to worry about."

Morris's great grin of derision shone on him. "It would be horrible," he said; "I expect you couldn't keep your mind off her if you had one. Never mind, think of your children in all parts of the world, then. What'll it be? Heads?"

Mr. Eberly carried a revolver in his pocket but he found no use for it. On the appalling tilt of the prom-enade-deck one felt unpleasantly shut in, seeing only the pale heavens, the fast eastward drift of the melting scud to starboard; only the long jostling slide of gray water getting green to port. From above came the dull sound of boots and men working, which was comforting. So was the undisturbed solidity of the ship. Even at this awkward angle the deck underfoot was firm as rock; the steel walls, white-painted, the windows, the heavy doors, looked strong and normal enough.

Mr. Eberly had all the passengers on deck now; the women and children in one compact group forward, ready for the boats which he presumed would be first down. At the after-rail, by the closed stairs, Mr. Sheedy waited, holding frankly an iron stanchion. He was watching the big Negroes of the black gang, who had either come up anyway or been sent up. They gathered, sullen, restless but impotent, about the hatch covers. They hadn't yet made any real movement to approach the promenade-deck. Mr. Eberly, moving with the aid of lines that he had rigged himself, passed up and down watching everybody; the groups of men smoking with affected calm; the confused herd of women where occasionally a child cried. He told them—he was careful not to do it too often—that there was absolutely no danger, and it was fine to see how they behaved; resigned, patient, doing exactly as they were asked. He had directed them to dress as warmly as possible, and he made sure that they had their ludicrous, bulky lifebelts on properly. Some of them managed to regard their appearance as amusing, and fortunately they were too ignorant to make any protest about a delay which Mr. Eberly himself found inexplicable, nerve-racking. Once he went inside with unhurried calm, waited a few minutes, and came out. "Assistance alongside in about an hour," he announced, with the well-sustained implication that he had been to the wireless-room.

Mr. Sheedy occasionally said, addressing the invisible deck aft: "Take your foot off the ladder, nigger, or you'll get a broken head." Then there was a faint stir, lasting only a minute; a slight acknowledgment of this obvious hint that some other people were not quite so calm. But they all knew, they had read or been told plenty of times, that the one real danger in matters like this was simply panic. Certainly they could see no other, now that they were used to the ship's position. They believed that men who understood the situation were doing everything possible to get them off quickly and safely; they had, in fact, nothing to worry about so long as they stayed quiet and did what Mr. Eberly directed them to do.

"Everything," asserted Mr. Eberly, who was still trying to explain to himself why Mr. Driscoll wasted so much time on the starboard boats, when it would have seemed fairly simple to Mr. Eberly to let go the port ones, "is all right."

Driven by his consuming anxiety, he finally did find a reason. The captain must consider it wiser to try to get off as many of the starboard boats as they could first. The port ones might be handled somewhat more expeditiously if later it proved that they were pressed for time. The idea, he told himself, had much to be said for it. He was heartened, too, by the indication it gave of confidence on the bridge that they would float a long while. With the impassivity of good discipline he refrained from sending above to make inquiries which could only be useless and ridiculous. "Try to be patient just a little longer," he said earnestly. "I know this isn't very comfortable, but there's no danger. The sun," he added with a sort of cheerfulness, "will be out in a minute."

From the well-deck forward Anthony could see Captain Clendening's stubborn, hatless white head against the sky. It was the one human detail in the confusion of the *San Pedro*'s superstructure. Insistently under Anthony's eyes the Negroes crouched against the cased automobiles. Their wide feet clung like stunted hands to the rivets of the deck-plates. Cords bulged out of their black necks; sweat trickled flashing under the wool on their skulls. Their enormous paws locked over levers; black hills of muscle humped across their straining shoulders; their eyes rolled white, their thick lips contracted.

Anthony looked at them through a fluctuating reddish mist. Weariness tightened his throat in rhythmic cramping retches. He would have spewed out his empty stomach if he could. Both his hands he had to keep behind him so he would not break an hysterical fist on the black stencil of an Indian's head, outstanding with the maker's name on the side of the case.

After a while he realized that men and muscle couldn't do it. They would never get that case over the side. It must be wedged. He cupped his hands and screamed to the bridge: "Let me go below and make MacGillivray give me steam on the winches, sir!"

He couldn't tell whether Captain Clendening heard him, whether the old man could hear anything, or understand if he did hear. The white head, stubbornly held up, wagged a little.

Anthony turned. "Drop that. Get up number two starboard boom—" There was no one, he saw, to whom he could safely delegate authority if he wanted intelligent action, but he picked out a man finally. "You," he said, "stand by to let in the valves. We'll get steam."

At the end, the Negro called Packy released his lever. His big hands pulled it out. One moment he poised on the tilted deck, his head sunk, his black jaw swung out.

Water raced up to his feet; his shoulders balanced. The steel bar drove like a battering-ram into the Indian's stenciled profile. Anthony wiped his forehead. His voice was thin as water. "Lay off that, nigger!"

The wood had splintered at the terrible impact. Pallid sunshine from the aching white sky with the washed clouds moving fell through the broken boards, winked on nickel, on smooth cream-colored enamel. That's an expensive car we're throwing away, thought Anthony.

He had removed his shoes to stand more securely. His feet, cold and wet in his torn socks, gave him a good grip on the slanting deck. The echo of the steel door closed behind him, and he forced himself to trot through the water in the alleyway. It caught his ankles and splashed at his knees; his unprotected heels falling hit his spine sickening jolts; and jarred beyond endurance, he had to stop, putting a hand, somehow worked raw, against the wall. He might have slept a moment, on his feet, to his shins in cold water, for he started, almost falling; remembered where he was going

Under a raw, thin fog of vapor the engine-room depths formed an infernal swimming-pool. Like monster green hogsheads the turbine cases rose in a fantastic steel swamp. Incredible vegetation flowered; white piping; flattened-out layers of open-work footways. Stairs edged with brass rail plunged down, leading nowhere. Heavy tanks; pistons in a stiff paralysis of the final failure of almost all the auxiliary systems; transparent oil-cups with the oil at an angle in them; everything seemed to have changed places in a mechan-

ical anarchy. Below, water moved about regularly, swaying to the sluggish roll. The engine-room shaft echoed
like a sea cave. Choking with a hundred tons of brine
in their throats the pumps groaned up to Anthony. Electric lights fluctuated, winked on the dirty sliding surface, steadied as the *San Pedro* came back. Anthony
stumbled down the iron slant of the ladder.

There was Mr. MacGillivray. He had the fire-room
door tied back, and the lock-door beyond fastened, too.
He braced himself between them, his eyes on the indicator dials and the bridge signal. Sometimes the water
came almost to his waist. Vapor slipped out steadily
above his head, licking the upper jamb. Anthony
missed a step, scraped his shin open, saw the bright
blood run on his foot before he landed in the water.
"Chief!"

Mr. MacGillivray snatched his arm. Anthony
shouted above the catch and gasp of the pumps: "I've
got to have steam."

Mr. MacGillivray's hanging cheeks were set into a
cold calm. Unavoidably retreating, he had lost almost
everything, but bitterly, step by step, he gave way in
grim good order, contesting each point with the invad-
ing ocean. His obdurate old face was wary, undismayed.
Anthony asked: "How much steam have you got, chief?"

Mr. MacGillivray's eyes came down from the dials.
"Eighty pounds!" he shouted. "The center boiler's
just gone. Listen to it!"

Over came the *San Pedro*, heavy and deliberate, rush-
ing water into the hot fire-box. It sounded like the
crash of thin metal sheets. The outlet valves whistled

harder in the darkness. Mr. MacGillivray shook his finger at the fire-room. "To their necks, some of them," he roared. "We can't stay much longer."

Anthony swayed against him, looking through. A naked black back with prodigious arms bent to ease down a coal-bucket. Water swayed toward its armpits. In the upper corner a door came wide, and violent yellow light spurted in shattered columns across the liquid surface. A great shadow moved; coal crashed in, iron rang on iron, and the light went out. Up came a white back this time, another bucket.

"Electricity gone there!" roared the chief. "Go everywhere in a minute. Tell the old man. The telephone doesn't work."

The black figure with the dangling arms waded past. His face, his conical skull swayed into the light; he grinned; he swung his apelike arm and wagged the hand up and down. A faint boom-boom came from his chest. "Home," he moaned, "knock on the door. . . ."

"My God," said Anthony, shocked, "he's singing."

"Sure! He's crazy!" shouted Mr. MacGillivray. "No one who wasn't crazy would be here. He's the only nigger left."

Anthony swallowed. "Give me pressure on a winch, chief. I got to get some cases over."

MacGillivray stared at him, open-mouthed. He laid a hand on his shoulder and shook him. "Wake up!" he roared. "Come to! You can't use your booms in this list. Tie 'em down before you hurt someone."

"I can try," Anthony said, "I got to—"

"You cannot!" bellowed MacGillivray, his amazement melted in anger. "Hell and damnation, where are your brains, boy? Are you all crazy? You aren't at dock! Did the old man put that up to you?"

"Maybe I can work it," said Anthony. "We've got to get those motors off. We—"

"Never mind them. You go up and find my fire-room crew. Tell the old man I got to have my men back." He shook Anthony's arm with a sort of fury. "Tell him they left. Tell him I got my engineers firing. Tell him if he wants to float to make those niggers come back here. Tell the old man we can't keep steam—tell him to come the hell down here himself!"

"He can't," shouted Anthony. "He's sick. He hasn't been to bed since Saturday night. What do you expect?"

"He's got no business to be sick," yelled MacGillivray. "Tell him I said so. Tell him we're foundering. Don't he give a damn? Don't he know we could capsize any minute? He'd lose every soul aboard. Just like that!" Mr. MacGillivray's loose fingers snapped soundless in the uproar. "Isn't he getting his passengers off?"

"We're doing everything we can," said Anthony. "We—"

"You are like hell!" roared MacGillivray. "Who's in command? The old man? He's dead to the world. Had him on the phone an hour ago and he didn't know what he was talking about! Why don't Driscoll take over? Why don't you take over? Are you so damn dumb you think you're going to float forever?"

"He's the master on this vessel," said Anthony. "As long as he's on the bridge giving orders, in the deck department we obey them. When we're ordered to

78

abandon, we'll abandon. Meanwhile we keep our mouths shut."

Mr. MacGillivray stared at him. Then he spat hard into the dirty water in front of Anthony. "Get out of here, brat! Believe me, if I was a sailor, I'd rather be drowned than have to tell people afterward what I was doing all morning. Jesus, I hope some of you get off alive!"

Anthony turned, but Mr. MacGillivray caught his shoulder suddenly. "Listen," he roared. "Tell the old man! Get it into him! Ask what he's doing with four hundred human beings somebody's going to want from us afterward. Tell him for Christ's sake use his head—"

Miro, still on the bridge, waiting for any further orders Captain Clendening might have, could not imagine what the men on the well-deck forward had in mind. He watched them release a boom from its cradle. Then they stood a moment apparently arguing. Then with a sort of feverish violence, they scrambled above, all laid hold on the cable, and struggling hard brought the boom up, jerk by jerk. It tilted, staggered, mounted uncertain toward the perpendicular. What must surely be the idiocy of this performance did not surprise Miro so much as the energy with which they went about it. They might, of course, be contemplating something which he did not understand, but he noted that Mr. Bradell was absent, and it seemed more likely that they were acting on their own initiative.

Not speaking, for he knew that the captain would not hear him, he came close and pointed insistently until

Captain Clendening looked. There was a long silence, and suddenly the captain, shaking his head a little, roared out: "On the fo'c'sle! Down that boom! What the devil is going on?"

Below, they wavered. Black faces turned. Out of the concealment of the deck-house under them came Mr. Bradell now, and he, too, turned. The boom hovered in a broken semicircle, balanced dizzily, went into a drunken side movement.

"Look alive, sir!" screamed Miro.

The boom, released, came too fast. With a blind, inert precision it swung farther left; the iron-sheathed timber struck like a well-directed club out of the anonymous skies. It knocked Mr. Bradell's poised figure ten feet into the scuppers. Up to them came the final crash of the demolished tip.

Captain Clendening opened his mouth and shut it. He shook his head and said: "Quartermaster?"

"Yes, sir," said Miro.

"Who was that?"

"Mr. Bradell, sir."

"Bradell," said Captain Clendening. "Bradell." He turned his head, continuing sharp and clearer: "Quartermaster."

"Yes, sir," said Miro, whiter.

"See about him." Captain Clendening's mustache worked stiffly. "Don't report back here. If he's alive, get him into a boat. Don't come back here. Get him away, get him off this ship. We're foundering."

"Yes, sir."

*

Left alone, Captain Clendening was quietly aware of death like a man beside him. He thought of his lungs bursting with sea water, a final agony of suffocation. This his body recoiled from, his gullet tightened, bitter saliva filling his mouth. He looked about carefully, as though there might be somewhere he could go; but it was a minute, never-completed gesture, for a habit of thought, an automatic pride, interrupted him. He was exposed, on the bridge; people could see him. The slugging of his heart, too large now for his chest, he could not control, but that was hidden. He knew perfectly how he had to die, and they did, too. He wished that they might for a moment face it; he would like to know —he was distracted, not ironic—if death would still seem so proper, so necessary, to them.

There his acuter senses broke down self-defensively. An anesthetic of poorer comprehension, a sort of mental stupor took off the momentary keen edge, veiled the face and fear of death. Deliberately, his hands heavy and inaccurate, he buttoned his bridge coat, tugged it into place. He made some motions to smooth the wrinkles from the sleeves, brushing the gold braid. After several uncertain efforts he picked up his uniform cap, and this, too, he brushed off, hitting it with his numb hand once or twice. Then he put it carefully on his head, brought the visor down, a stiff, somehow heartening, line across his vision. He stood as straight as he could, supporting himself when necessary on the rail.

From the south the sea was traveling in long swells. Miro, braced against the backboard of boat ten, supported Mr. Bradell between his knees. He did not know what time it was; he had somehow smashed his good watch. The glass was gone and the hands snapped off; there was sea water in it and some blood from Mr. Bradell's broken head. They had more than thirty Negroes on board, and this, Miro recognized, was shameful, but he could not prevent it while he had Mr. Bradell to look out for, and he told himself that if they had been the first to cut loose, he had orders to get away. Many of the other boats had been filled; one, he saw—and it frightened him more than anything else—was entirely filled with women and children. He tried to call Mr. Fenton's attention to the fact that there was no one in it capable of managing it. What would they do? Mr. Fenton paid no attention to him, and the men in number ten, mutinous at the delay, pushed off; with great difficulty got clear. Miro hoped that it might at least set the others an example; that they wouldn't wait any longer for an order to abandon. Otherwise, he understood, they might sink where they were, boats still attached, many people still on deck.

Mr. Bradell moved between his knees and Miro was seized with distress and consternation, for it occurred to him that now Mr. Bradell would realize that number ten had deliberately drawn off, leaving hundreds of people in danger of death. He said at once: "Captain's orders to abandon, sir."

Anthony's face had fallen apart, but it was bound up fairly well with a handkerchief and a hard web of pain. He did not realize anything; and not knowing how he got where he was, where he had been, or for how long, Anthony made an effort to learn the time. The left arm with his wrist-watch he found to be no longer subject to his control. Pain of light on his eyes made him look up, and by the thin sun hung above him in the white sky he knew that it was close to noon. The boat, riding roughly, passed up a mound of water and let him see, amazed, the *San Pedro*.

He was stupefied by this sight. He had seen the *San Pedro* too often; he recognized at once that this view of her was a dream. It was impossible, it would be fatal. She could not remain like that. Here was no matter ballast-tanks could correct—her list was mortal, and at once he heard a low voice saying: *"But you do not float quite level. . . ."*

He started to make a movement, to arise; and hands were instantly on him, holding him. Blood came into his mouth. A scalding void complemented his body, filling out the electric emptiness where half his face and all his shoulder should have been. Waves of heat overpowered him—so strong that with them came the imaginary smell of hot oil, the roar of the engine-room shaft. At his side, in a shabby black overcoat, he saw the horrid author of that low voice, insistent, plucking at him: *"But you do not float . . ."*

This, he knew, was entirely false; he saw, actually, nothing but the men forward, the gunwales, the mounting green water; literal things in a spinning blur of fever and pain—yet, in a way, Doctor Percival remained; the fleshless face was steady and close, brooding on them.

83

Seeing thus, while not seeing, he smelt stronger than salt and blood the warmed sweetness of patchouli; he was aware of the dark, despairing blue of her eyes, the frail flippancy of her voice like a veil drawn decently over her unspeakable desire to live.

Then, violently, without escape, he knew that this was real, not a dream. The *San Pedro* was really there; the ocean was in her; the sea smothered her tremendous engines. It choked up every passage and part of her; swamped into silence the marvelous elaboration of her machines, quenched all her lights, and would in a moment drag her down like any broken metal. Water would do away quickly with everything that breathed aboard her. The boat brought him up again. Cold as he had been hot, he saw once more the *San Pedro*.

Just adequately the *San Pedro* met each swell; no wasted effort. She lay on her port side, down by the head, and took her terrible rest while the mounds of water pillowed her and washed her quietly. Like the disarray of weariness, starboard davits on the top deck dangled out trailing ropes, suspended white boats unevenly. Expiring wisps of steam broke in curls from her flanks. She had a screw clear, pinned like a mighty metal flower on the slim cone of the starboard bracket.

There she lay in a motionless lethargy, and then without pause or warning, she went. The shooting swell rose in a hill, came quite over her bows. Her funnel inclined; water poured freely into it, into the high hoods of her ventilators. Deep in her, a hidden drum boom-boomed. Like a pool, the dark gully of her promenade-deck filled forward; steam mounted in columns through her coal-hatches. A great metallic sigh, a six-hundred-foot shudder—why hadn't her boilers blown, lifted thunderous through her exhausted sides?—she was going home, going to some deep sleep. The waters folded over her tumultuously—air, steam, the great chords booming in her hull. . . .

There remained Anthony, harassed by great pain, the boat under him, Miro behind him, the black men with the oars; if there were other boats, he could not see them. Only, overhead, the vast sky, pale and white, all around the infinite empty ocean.